MW00951026

Chickens Don't Wear Tutus!

Laura Willingham

The Blue Ridge Barn was having its annual Moonlight Chicken Dance.
This was the biggest event of the year.

But a young chicken named Lily was very sad.
She did not want to attend the dance.

"I don't have many feathers," fretted Lily.
Mom reminded Lily that she was young,
and her feathers would soon grow.

"There must be something I can do," Lily pondered.
She rummaged through the house looking for something to create.
"I need to make my feathers look full and fluffy."

She pulled down the blue mosquito net that draped over her bed.

She cut and sewed and cut and sewed.
"Perfect!" she shouted.

Lily beamed with joy as she put on her tutu.

When Mom walked into the room, she saw Lily in her tutu.
"Chickens don't wear tutus!" she stated.

"They do now," responded Lily.
"You look pretty!" said Mom.

Mom suddenly felt sad.
"My feathers look dull and worn out," she sighed.

Lily got very busy. She pulled down the purple mosquito net that draped over Mom's chaise lounge.

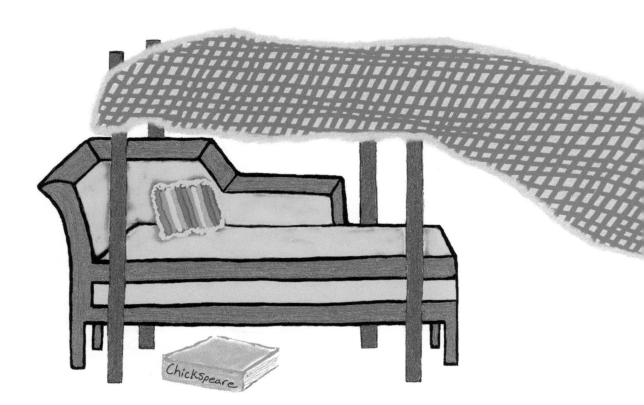

She cut and sewed and cut and sewed.
"Perfect!" she shouted.

"Look Mom. I made you a tutu!"

Mom beamed with joy as she put on her tutu.

When Dad arrived home, he saw Lily and Mom twirling around in their tutus! "Chickens don't wear tutus!" he stated. "They do now," responded Lily and Mom.

"Don't we look pretty for the dance tonight?" Lily asked.
"You look pretty!" Dad replied.

Dad suddenly felt sad.
"My feathers are grey, and I feel old," he sighed.

Lily got very busy. She pulled down the red mosquito
net that draped over the porch hammock.
She cut and sewed and cut and sewed.
"Perfect!" she shouted.

"Look Dad. I made you a tutu!"

Dad beamed with joy as he put on his tutu.

When they arrived at the annual Moonlight Dance,
the hostess Miss Betsy greeted them.
"Chickens and roosters don't wear tutus!" she stated.

"They do now," responded Lily, Mom, and Dad.

When they entered the dance,
everyone stared at them in awe!

Lily, Mom, and Dad walked onto the dance floor and twirled the night away and never again was it said that chickens don't wear tutus!

About the Author

Laura Willingham is a native of North Carolina. She is currently living on Monkey Island at Grand Lake in Oklahoma with her husband Barry and dog named Willie. Her purpose for writing and illustrating is to provide children with a moment of joy.

Outside of writing, she enjoys running, hiking, and spending time with family and friends.

BLACK ROSE
writing™

All rights reserved. No part of this book may be reproduced, stored in a retrieval system or transmitted in any form or by any means without the prior written permission of the publishers, except by a reviewer who may quote brief passages in a review to be printed in a newspaper, magazine or journal.

The final approval for this literary material is granted by the author.

First printing

This is a work of fiction. Names, characters, businesses, places, events and incidents are either the products of the author's imagination or used in a fictitious manner. Any resemblance to actual persons, living or dead, or actual events is purely coincidental.

ISBN: 978-1-944715-86-1 (Hardcover)
PUBLISHED BY BLACK ROSE WRITING
www.blackrosewriting.com

© 2021 by Laura Willingham

Printed in the United States of America

CPSIA information can be obtained
at www.ICGtesting.com
Printed in the USA
BVHW022248290821
615463BV00001B/1

9 781944 715861